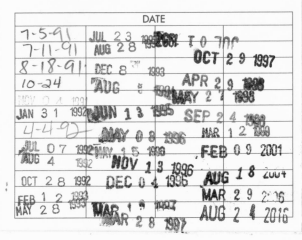

The POTATO MAN

Story by Megan McDonald
Pictures by Ted Lewin

Orchard Books   New York

For Mom and Dad who gave me the story
　　M.M.

In memory of Ben the Huckster
　　T.L.

————————————————————

Orchard Books, A division of Franklin Watts, Inc.
387 Park Avenue South, New York, NY 10016

Manufactured in the United States of America. Printed by General
Offset Company, Inc. Bound by Horowitz/Rae. Book design by
Mina Greenstein. The text of this book is set in 16 pt. ITC
Bookman Light. The illustrations are watercolor paintings.
10 9 8 7 6 5 4 3 2 1

Library of Congress Cataloging-in-Publication Data
McDonald, Megan. The potato man. "A Richard Jackson book"—
Summary: Grandpa tells stories of the fruit and vegetable
huckster in his childhood neighborhood, a man he learns to
appreciate after a rocky start. [1. Peddlers and peddling—
Fiction] I. Lewin, Ted, ill. II. Title
PZ7.M478419Po 1991 [E] 90-7758
ISBN 0-531-05914-6 ISBN 0-531-08514-7 (lib.)

"Here's how it happened," Grampa began:

Me and Otto were playin' a game of Run Sheep Run the day we first saw the Potato Man. He had only one eye, and his face, why, it was as lumpy as a potato itself.

In those days, lots of people came down East Street
fixin' and sellin' things, right up to your front door even.

Whenever I heard "Knives! Knives and scissors heee-re!" I grabbed Mama's kitchen shears and waited out on the front porch for the knife sharpener. I loved watchin' his grindstone whirr, sparks flyin' off the old wheel.

Best of all was the organ-grinder. He strolled down our hill playin' "Pop Goes the Weasel" on his hurdy-gurdy. When the music went POP! his lovebird, Rascal, would hand you a fortune in his beak:

YOU WILL HAVE THREE TIMES GOOD LUCK.

I remember the day I got that fortune, because it should'a said "three times BAD luck." That was the same day the Potato Man first came ridin' down East Street in his horse-drawn wagon, reins crackin' like a snapped twig, callin' "Abba-no-potata-man!"

That's how we named him the Potato Man. He was the new huckster, come sellin' fruits and vegetables—apples, potatoes, turnips, rutabagas, cabbages piled high in his wagon.

"Abba-no-potata-man!" he yelled loud as anything.

My dog Dukie almost broke his chain barkin' at him. I could hear my sisters jumpin' rope:

> *Rutabaga Rosie*
> *Eyes like posies . . .*

but they dropped their rope and ran all the way home when they saw his one eye.

I hid in the toolshed. Mama always gave me a nickel to get four bananas for us, but I didn't buy any that day, not one. I stayed right there and listened to the rain on the tin roof.

Before supper, Mama was peelin' potatoes, cuttin' away the bad spots, tellin' my sisters there was nothin' to be afraid of—it was just old Mr. Angelo who lost his right eye in the Great War.

The kids started yellin' "Abba-no-potata-man!" at him whenever he came around. They chased after his wagon, throwin' cinders at the back of it.

Then the bad luck started.

First was when a pile of potatoes bounced off his wagon. Me and Otto picked them up and hid them in our coat pockets. We built a fire behind the toolshed and roasted them on sticks.

"We shouldn'a taken these," Otto told me. "It's stealin'."

"Potato Man's half blind. He couldn'a saw us," I told him back.

But he saw all right. Told Mama I was worse'n a ground squirrel, too. She had me peelin' potatoes every night for a week.

Second time, I squeezed a whole orange in my sister's hair when she wasn't lookin'. She ran out of the house screamin', flies buzzin' all around her head. There was the Potato Man sittin' in his wagon, watchin' the whole thing.

Mama got me good for that one, too, but it didn't stop me from callin' my sister "Old Flypaper" for the longest while.

That was two times bad luck.

After that, Otto and me were sneakin' into the Shaeffer yard one day, climbin' on their garage to peek through a crack in the roof at their shiny new Stanley Steamer.

If *he* hadn't yelled "Abba-no-potata-man!" just then, givin' me a start, my foot wouldn'a slipped and broke the window.

Bad luck times three, that's what that was.

"Maybe the bad luck's about over," Otto was sayin'. Like a splinter finally workin' its way out.

"Potato Man can't be comin' round much anymore. Too cold."

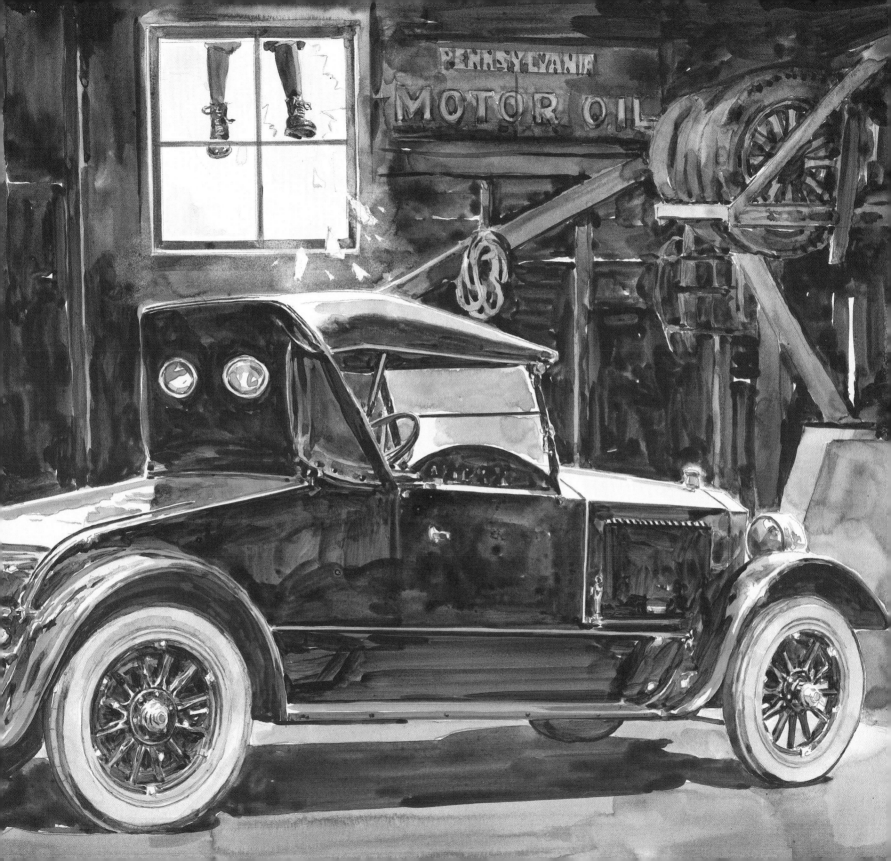

Next thing I knew, first real snow's fallin'. Me and Otto were out catchin' snowflakes when I heard Dukie barkin' like crazy from down the street.

Up close, I saw Dukie had a bright red ball in his mouth. Seemed like the Potato Man wanted it.

"Drop it, Dukie! Dukie! Drop it!" I yelled. "Here, boy. Give it here, Dukie!" I called, comin' up on him. Dukie dropped it in my hand.

An Indian apple!

I looked at the round, red pomegranate all nice and shiny, and just knew it was the Potato Man's.

I figured three times bad luck was enough for me. So I walked over to him and looked him right in his good eye.

His eye twitched. He pushed back his wool cap and I could see his whole face quiver, gettin' ready to yell at me somethin' awful.

"This yours?" I asked, handin' it over.

"No, sonny," the Potato Man mumbled. His eye shut and opened almost like a wink. "I do believe it's yours. Merry Christmas to ya, too."

He climbed back in his wagon and yelled "Heeee-yah!" slappin' those reins.

Winter came for good, and that's the last we heard "Abba-no-potata-man" for a time. . . .

"Say it again, Grampa. Say about the Potato Man again."

"Did he come back, Grampa? Did you see the Potato Man ever after that?"

"Old Mr. Angelo? He came back that next spring, and the next one, for as long as I remember growin' up on East Street. Once even sold me the biggest pumpkin you ever did see."

"Tell us about it, Grampa."

"Tell us another one about when you were a boy."

"Not tonight. Tomorrow. Tomorrow's another story."